An Eggstra-Special Easter!

By Matt Huntley • Illustrated by Jason May

Random House New York

AMEET Sp. z o.o.
Nowe Sady 6, 94-102 Łódź—Poland
ameet@ameet.eu
www.ameet.eu

www.LEGO.com

Published in the United States by Random House Children's Books, a division of Penguin Random House LLC, 1745 Broadway, New York, NY 10019, and in Canada by Penguin Random House Canada Limited, Toronto. Random House and the colophon are registered trademarks of Penguin Random House LLC.
rhcbooks.com
ISBN 978-0-593-43178-8 (trade) — ISBN 978-0-593-48107-3 (ebook)
Printed in the United States of America
10 9 8 7 6 5 4 3 2 1

One warm, sunny day, Duncan stepped out of his house and smiled. Flowers were blooming. Tomorrow was Easter, and that was Duncan's favorite day of the year.

"This is going to be the best Easter ever," he announced. "I need to get ready."

Duncan started decorating his home with garlands of fresh flowers.

Next was planning the town egg hunt. And, of course, he had to dust off his bunny costume.

Duncan was also excited to watch his neighbor prepare. It was possible that his neighbor liked Easter even more than he did. His neighbor was . . . the Easter Bunny.

But something was odd. The Easter Bunny's carrot-shaped house was quiet. There should have been piles of colorful eggs and baskets of flowers on her lawn, ready to be delivered. Duncan didn't even hear the whir of the egg-painting machine.

He went over there to make sure nothing was wrong.

POST

When the Easter Bunny opened the door, she didn't look happy. And she was using a crutch.

"Is everything okay?" Duncan asked.

"I'm afraid not," the Easter Bunny admitted. "I was doing my hopping exercises this morning, and I hurt my foot. I can't get my eggs ready, and there's no way I can deliver my baskets tomorrow. I don't think there will be an Easter this year."

Duncan couldn't believe his ears.

"There has to be something we can do," he said.

The Easter Bunny shrugged sadly, but then she had an idea. "Maybe you could help! You could finish the eggs and deliver them. You could be the Easter Bunny this year! You even have a nifty bunny suit."

Duncan didn't know what to say. This was a very important job. Could he do it?

"I can do it!" he declared. "At least, I think I can."

"That would be a great help." The Easter Bunny looked relieved. "Let's get you started."

Duncan followed her as she limped into her backyard.

"This is the egg-painting machine," the Easter Bunny said, pushing a button. The big machine started to hum. "Over there are the baskets."

"This seems pretty easy," said Duncan. "I'll take care of everything for you. Don't worry."

"Thank you," said the Easter Bunny. "Now I need to rest my aching foot."

She went back into her house, and Duncan started to work.

Eggs began rolling out of the machine. But it was going very slowly—and all the eggs were orange!

Duncan wasn't sure what to do. He didn't want to disturb the tired bunny. He wanted to prove that he could do this himself.

Duncan cautiously pushed some buttons on the machine and turned a dial.

The machine started to shake and make strange noises. *Whirrr-pitt-pitt-pitt*. The orange eggs were popping out of the machine faster and faster.

"Oh, no!" Duncan exclaimed. "I have to stop this!"

He pushed more buttons and turned the dial again.

The machine began to make more strange noises.

Zing-zing-zing! Bonk-bonk-bonk!

Then the machine stopped rolling out eggs and started making all sorts things. There were soccer balls and swim fins, bicycle wheels and canoe paddles.

Duncan turned the dial back and forth. More items rolled off the conveyor belt. There were skis and a tent, skateboards and guitars, hats, wrenches, and a bullhorn. Finally, the machine shuddered and stopped.

"What have I done?" Duncan said to himself. "I only made a few orange eggs and a bunch of other stuff. This isn't very Eastery."

But he had promised that he would be the Easter Bunny this year. He had to deliver the eggs and gifts.

As the sun was rising on Easter morning, Duncan brushed off his bunny costume and put it on. Then he loaded his baskets and treats onto a wagon, hooked the wagon to his scooter, and zoomed off.

Duncan rode all around town, leaving gifts on people's doorsteps.

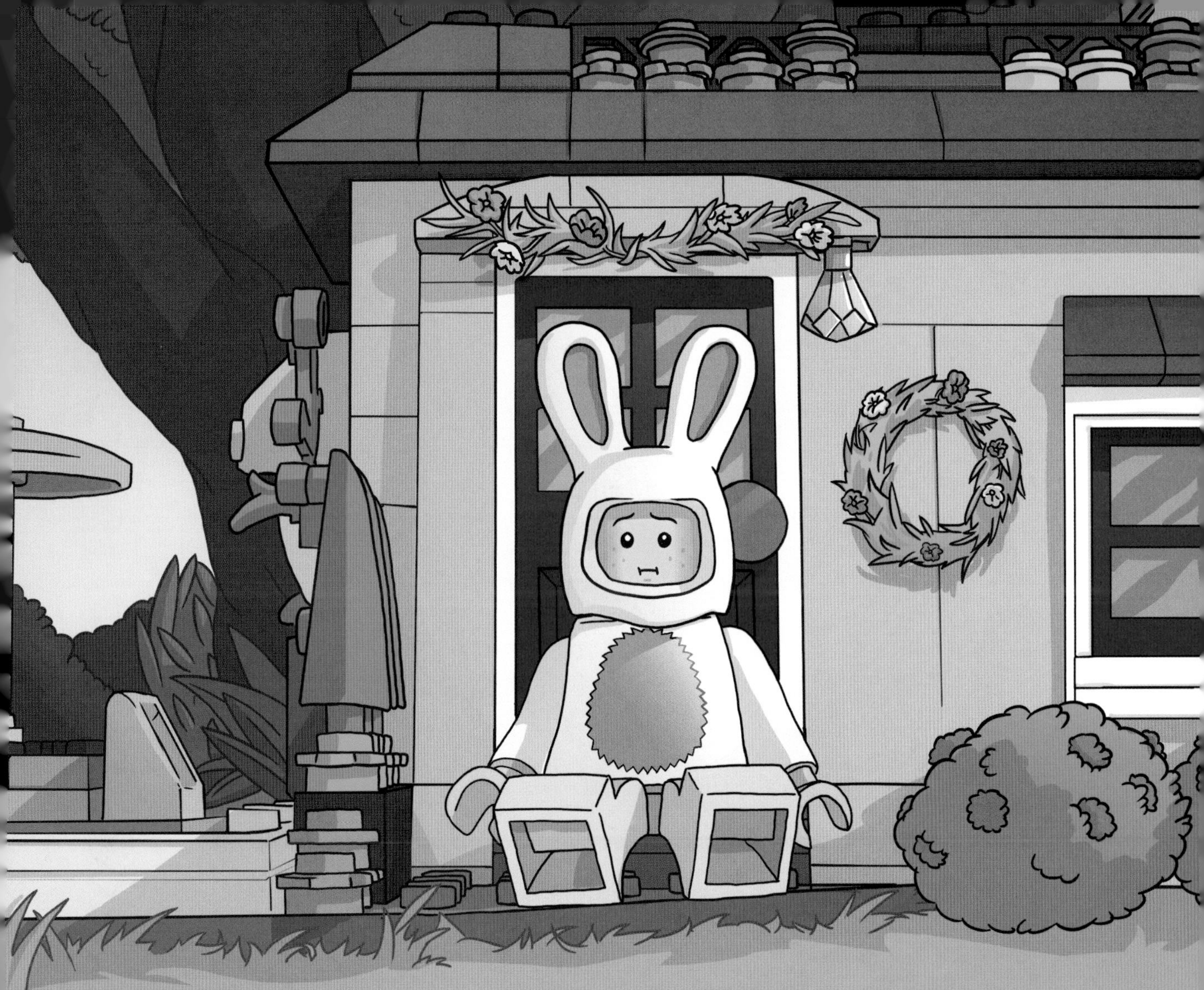

When Duncan was finished, he went home and sat on his porch. He was very tired and not sure he had done a good job. He was worried that he had ruined Easter.

Just then, he heard voices. Townspeople were coming down the street.

"Did you deliver the baskets this morning?" asked a woman holding a swim fin.

"Yes, I'm sorry," Duncan said. He started to explain about the Easter Bunny's foot and the egg-painting machine breaking down.

"Sorry?" the woman said. "We wanted to thank you. I lost a fin and needed a new one. It was the perfect gift."

"These tires are just what we need to finish building our go-kart," one boy said. His friend nodded.

"We swapped our gifts," a happy girl said. "I always wanted a skateboard."

"And I needed new wrench," a woman added.

"We love your bunny costume!" a man announced. "You inspired us to make our own Easter outfits. I'm a butterfly."

"I'm a flower," his friend declared.

"This is wonderful news," Duncan said. "I was worried that I had ruined everyone's Easter."

"Ruined it?" said the woman with the wrench. "You saved Easter! And I bet if we work together, we can fix the egg-painting machine with my new wrench."

The townspeople cheered and went to work. They tightened bolts and adjusted pipes. They even added a giant claw to help distribute baskets.

When they were done, the egg-painting machine glistened and gleamed and hummed like new. It now made colorful eggs . . . as well as surprise gifts.